Lois Ehlert

Rain Fish

Beach Lane Books • New York London Toronto Sydney New Delhi

When blue sky turns gray

and it rains all day,

that's when rain fish come out

and play.

They hide in debris

until rain sets them free.

Do you see them, too?

or is it just me?

They love to splash in puddles

and dance

upon concrete.

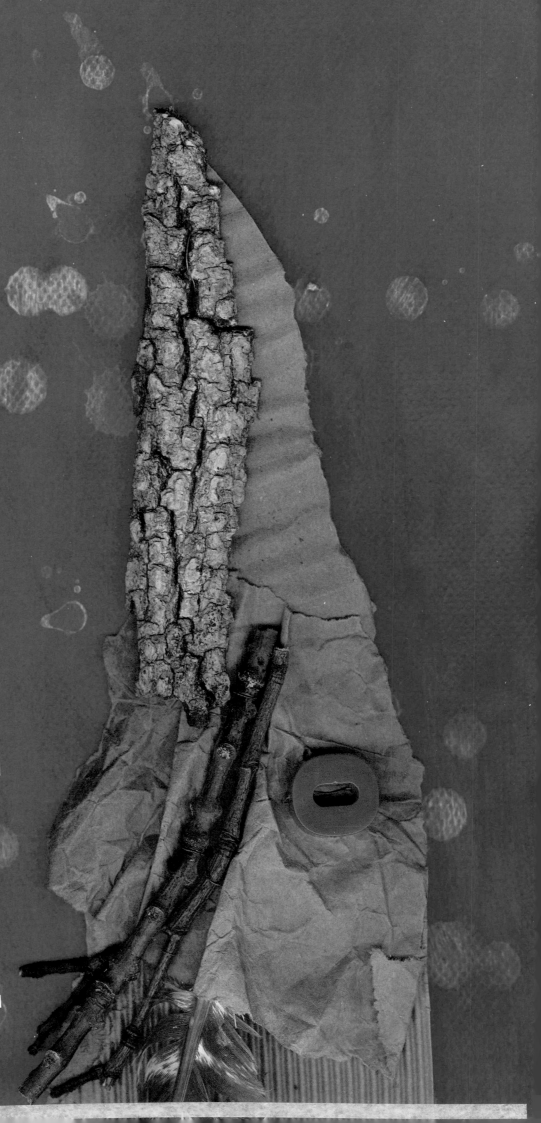

They gather

and then swish on down the street.

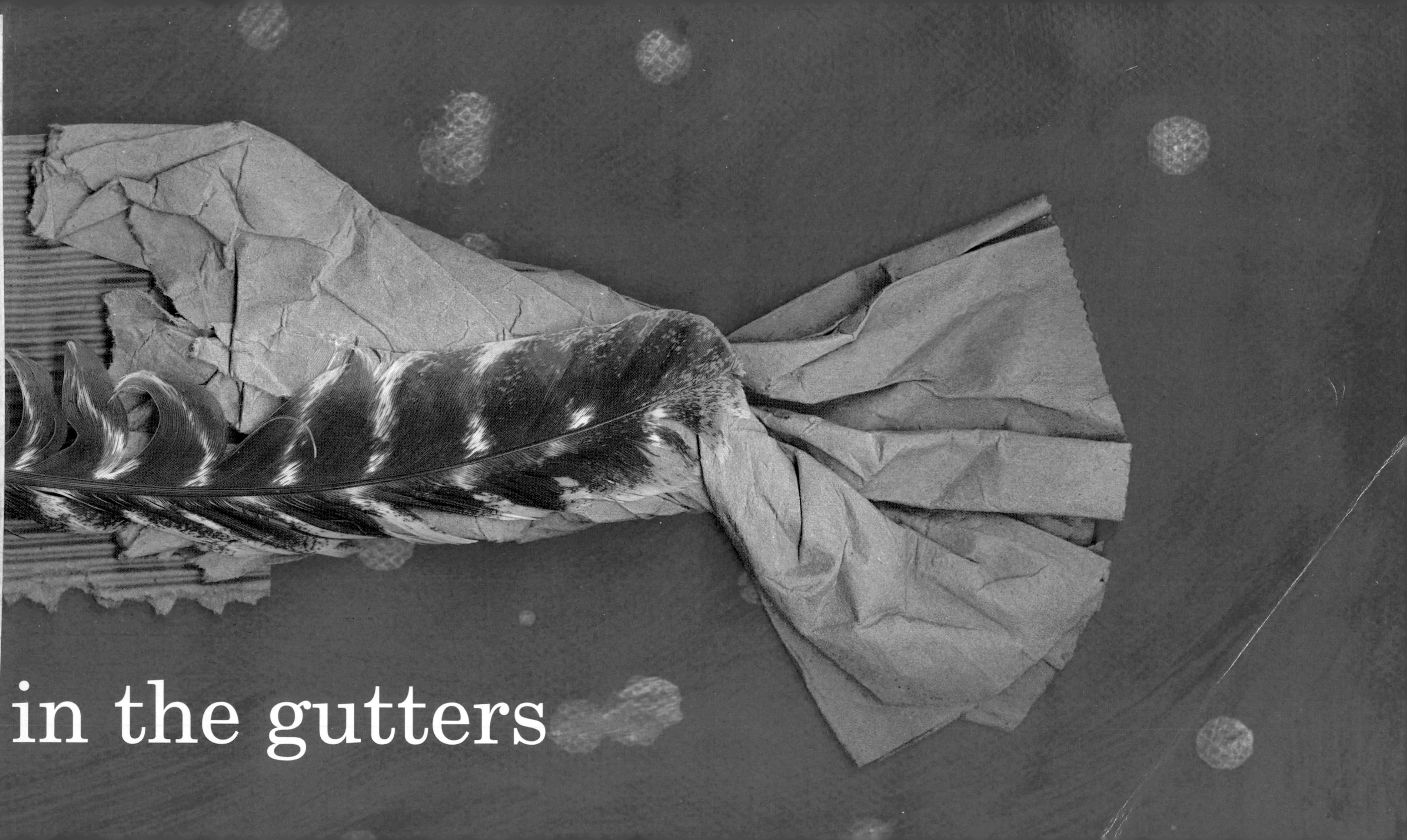

in the gutters

DO NO[T] BEND

CALENDAR SUBMISSIONS

Send information for TV Weekend calendar

Elaine Rewolinski
Journal Sentinel
P.O. Box 371
Milwaukee 53201-0371

Information also may be faxed to (414) 224-3 or e-mailed kxndclue@journalsentinel.co/... Include a street address for ... events must be sent weekly... writing by 8 a.m. one week... telephone. No listing cal... calendar only.

The Jazz Estate: The
Elementals, 9:30 p.m. Nov.
28, 2423 N. Murray Ave.

Pete Lange/Gary Meisner
Jazz Quartet, 6-9 p.m. De...

O'Donoghue's Irish Pub:
...Guire's: Up All
...0 p.m. Nov. 23, 5... than Christ...
...7th St. Hales Corner...
...s Sports Dock Joe...and be...

Elementals, 9:30...
p.m. Nov. 29, Honeyboy's
Jazz Trio open jazz session,
8:30 p.m. Dec. 4, 401 S. 2nd
St.

...n Spencer Band, 9:30
...p.m. Nov. 23...
...wauk Franklin, craft...
Corn featurin... Creek Comm...
...e: Thanf rom...
Gran...kee Nov. 30, 600...
...givins along water... Nov.,
Roge Swampto... 3 p.m. Nov. 2...
G3 26, W985 ...ell Ave. Oak C...
...enter Drive,
...owoc Villag...

But you better look fast,

PLEASE
HANDLE WITH CARE

0:3/6656/1/9966/1

THIS SIDE

PACKING LIST ENCLOSED

Item

because rain fish don't last.

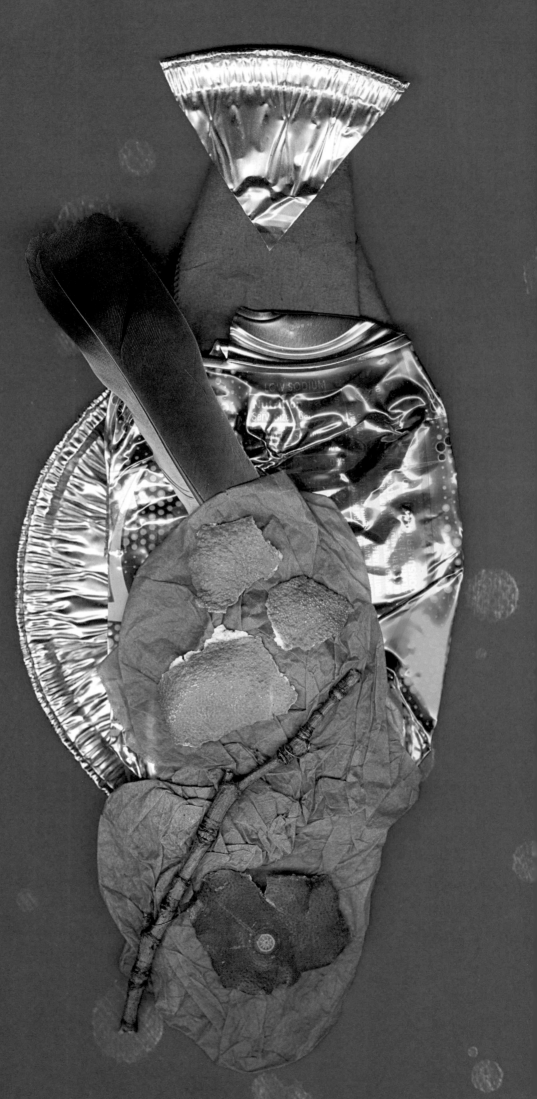

One day they're near,

the next, they disappear.

I wonder where they go from here.

If I I had a fish tail,

DO NOT B...

Aid 42144

I'd swim to warm seas,

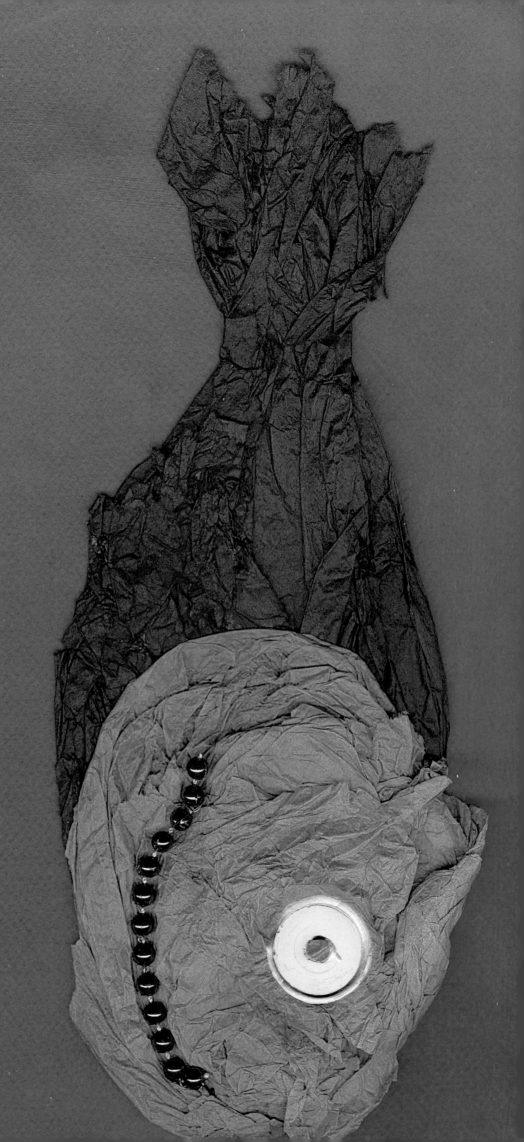

where new friends and palm trees

DO NOT BEND

would wave to greet me.

Sailors see rain fish, at least

A10 42144

that's what they say.

But when they try to catch them,

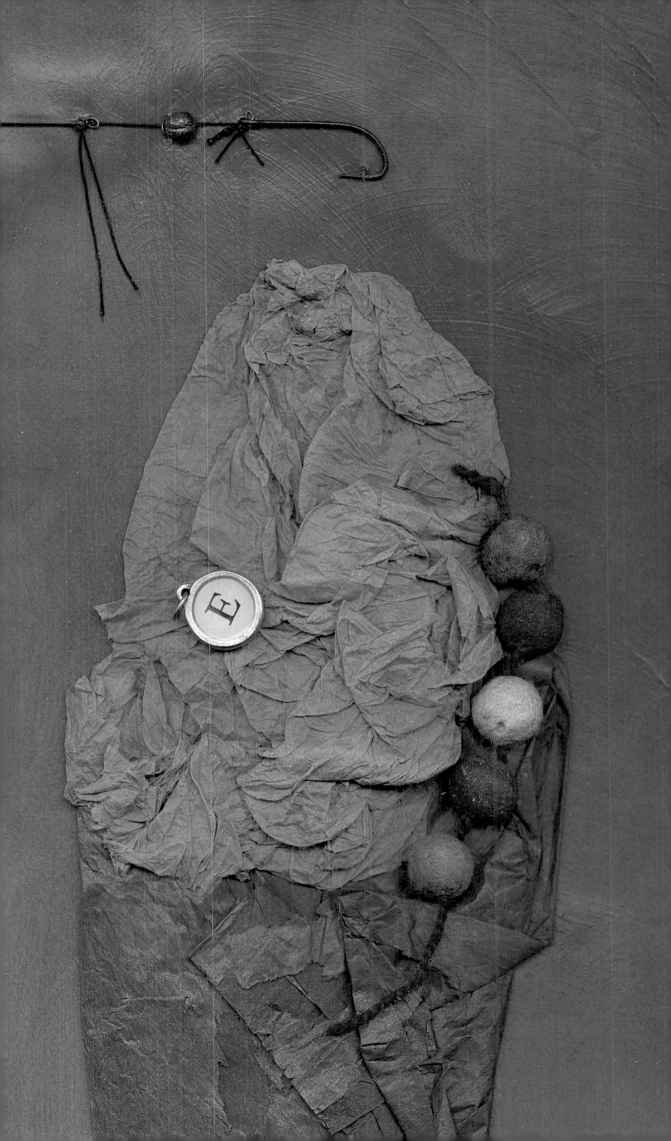

rain fish always . . . .

swim away swim away.

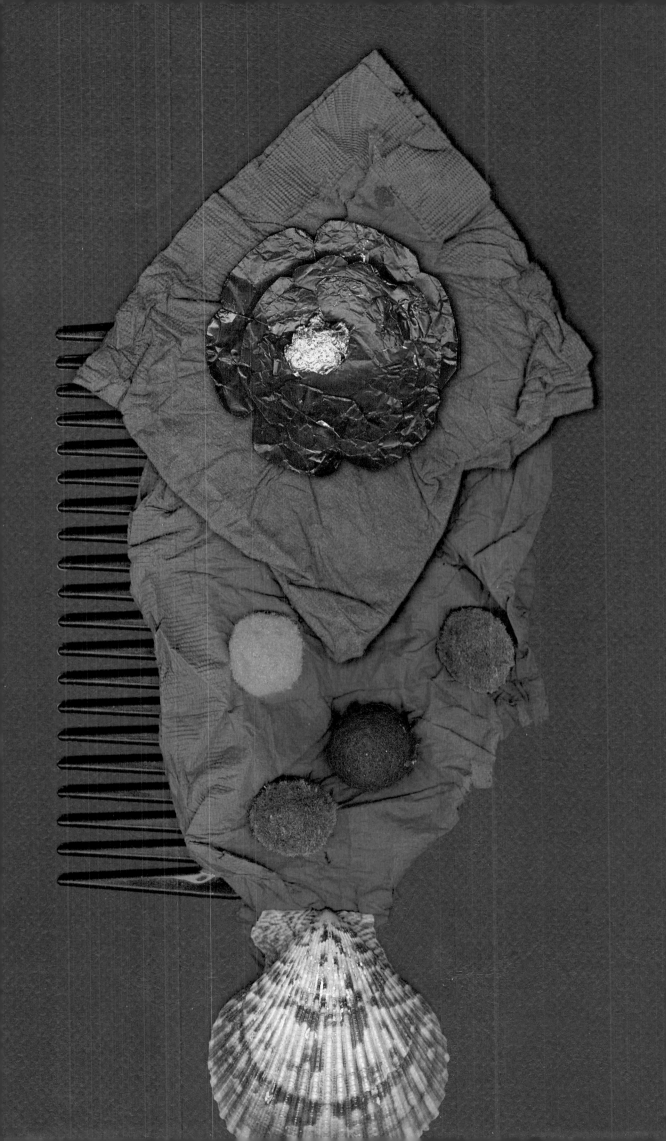

fish bobber

necklace

charm

twig

box top

paper plate

feather

plastic letter

can top

purse

orange peel